Princess
Katie's
Kittens

Books by Julie Sykes

Princess Katie's Kittens

Pixie at the Palace
Bella at the Ball
Suki in the Snow
Poppy and the Prince
Ruby and the Royal Baby

Woodland Magic

Fox Cub Rescue
Deer in Danger
The Stranded Otter
Operation Owl

Princess Katie's Kittens

Pixie at the Palace

Julie Sykes

Illustrated by Sam Loman

Piccadilly
PRESS

First published in Great Britain in 2012 by Piccadilly Press

This edition published in 2023 by
PICCADILLY PRESS
4th Floor, Victoria House, Bloomsbury Square, London WC1B 4DA
Owned by Bonnier Books, Sveavägen 56, Stockholm, Sweden
www.piccadillypress.co.uk

A CIP catalogue record for this book is available from the British Library.

ISBN: 978-1-80078-531-1

Also available as an ebook

1

Typeset by Envy Design Ltd

Printed and bound in Great Britain by Clays Ltd, Elcograf S.p.A.

Piccadilly Press is an imprint of Bonnier Books UK
| www.bonnierbooks.co.uk

For Gladys and Joe – J.S.

For Annabelle Jolie,
my own fluffy cat – S.L.

1

A Journey

The silver Rolls-Royce stopped outside Starlight Palace and Princess Katie of Tula unfastened her seatbelt.

'Thank you for picking me up, Mr Bentley.'

'You're welcome, Princess. Homework now, is it?'

'We didn't get any today so I'm free to go riding!'

Princess Katie bubbled with excitement. She loved horses and had her own pony, a dapple-grey mare called Misty. Katie visited Misty every day, even though being a princess meant that she was sometimes too busy to ride her.

Mr Bentley held open the car door as Katie picked up her school bag and climbed out. A fluffy white Persian cat was sitting on the stone steps that led up to the palace.

'Hello, Crystal,' said Katie, stretching out her hand.

Crystal stared back, haughtily twitched her whiskers, then stood up and walked away.

Katie sighed. She'd been trying to stroke Crystal ever since she was a tiny kitten, but the royal cat was very choosy about her friends. The only time she let Katie touch her was if she wanted feeding.

'I wish you were a cuddly cat!' called Katie. 'I'd let you sleep on my bed.'

Crystal kept walking and Katie swallowed her disappointment. Never mind. At least Misty was always pleased to see her, even though the pony was too big to sleep in her bedroom. Giggling at the thought, Katie hurried indoors.

The silver-grey kitten with black stripes peered round the table leg. His sisters were lying together in their basket. Silently, he crept towards them, dodging behind the bin when his tortoiseshell sister turned her head. Had she seen him? He stood very still until she settled down, yawned lazily and closed her orange eyes. Bunching his tiny body, the kitten pounced and landed in the basket on top of everyone.

At once, his tortoiseshell sister sprang up, hissing in surprise, claws drawn.

'Got you!' the kitten giggled.

'Meow!' The tortoiseshell kitten cuffed him playfully.

His other sisters – one white, one black and white and one grey and white – jumped on his back.

The kitten squeaked with pleasure. He loved a good play fight. Rolling about, he batted at everyone with his paws and tail.

The fun lasted ages until, suddenly, all the kittens ran out of energy. They flopped down in their basket, their tiny bodies squashed together so it was impossible to tell where one kitten ended and the next began.

We're getting bigger, thought the silver-grey kitten sleepily. Soon their mother would take them outside and teach them how to hunt. He could hardly wait! Mum told exciting stories of the

great outdoors. She was an excellent hunter, which was lucky, as there was never enough to eat at home.

'Our owner, Mrs Baxter, doesn't mean to let us go hungry,' Mum told the kittens. 'She's old and doesn't have much money.'

Mum was out hunting now. Each day she left the kittens alone for a little longer, preparing them for the day when they would be old enough to go out into the world by themselves.

A door opened and Mrs Baxter shuffled in, carrying a large box with black marks on the outside. Ears pricked, the kitten sat up. This looked interesting.

Mrs Baxter put the box on the floor and gave him a sad smile. 'Hello, little one. Have you just woken up?' Slowly, she bent down and scratched the kitten behind his pixie-like ears.

That was so good! Purring with delight, he rubbed his head against her knobbly fingers. Something wet splashed on his head.

Ew! He didn't like that!

Indignantly, he shook it away. The wet stuff was leaking from Mrs Baxter's eyes. Was she all right?

The kitten had never seen that happen before.

Mrs Baxter sniffed, pulled a tissue from her pocket and blew her nose loudly.

'I'm sorry. I wish I didn't have to do this. I can't afford to keep you and I don't know where to go for help. I'll leave you somewhere safe. You'll be away from the road but in a place where lots of people walk. Someone will find you. They'll give you a better home than I can.'

The kitten was baffled. What did she mean? He meowed in protest as Mrs Baxter lifted him by the scruff of his neck, supporting his bottom with her hand, and gently put him into the box. Sheets of newspaper lined the floor. It wasn't as cosy as the kitten's basket and it rustled when he moved, but it was comfortable enough. Then he heard a frightened squeak. That was his black-and-white sister. The silver-grey kitten jumped at the sides of the box, wanting to climb out and comfort her.

'Easy there. I'm not leaving you on your own.' Mrs Baxter lowered his four sisters in beside him.

'What's going on?' they squealed.

'It's all right. She's not going to hurt us.' The kitten busied himself licking everyone, like Mum did, until they'd calmed down.

Suddenly, the box began to wobble. Mrs Baxter grunted as she struggled to lift it. The kittens pricked their ears in alarm, but the silver-grey kitten remembered that Mrs Baxter was always kind.

'She'll be taking us somewhere nice,' he said confidently.

They travelled in a car. The kitten knew about cars from Mum. She'd told him never to run in front of them and not to fall asleep inside one either, because then you might get lost. Mrs Baxter had put a lid on the box. It was dark, with only a few small holes to let in air.

The kitten's green eyes widened as they adjusted to the gloom. He peered through a hole, but it wasn't

big enough to see through. He sat up
straight, ears pricked as he tried to
follow the direction they were taking,
but it was a bumpy ride and he soon
got confused. Sighing softly, the kitten
lay down with his sisters.

A long while later, the drive was
over. As Mrs Baxter lifted the box out
of the car, the kitten's nose twitched
with excitement. What was that
delicious smell? It was the same scent
that clung to Mum when she'd been
out hunting. It tickled his nose and
made him want to run and jump.

Suddenly, he remembered what it was. It was the smell of the great outdoors! It was the place Mum called the woods.

The kitten purred with excitement. 'We're in a forest.'

He could hardly sit still. He wished Mrs Baxter would hurry up. She was walking slowly and he couldn't wait to get out of the box and explore his new surroundings.

At last, Mrs Baxter stopped and carefully lowered the box to the ground. Pulling back a corner of the lid, she stroked each kitten on the head.

'Good luck,' she whispered.

The kitten rubbed his head against her hand. As she pulled away, he glimpsed a tall tree stretching above him. The lid closed suddenly.

'Wait,' he cried in frustration.

But all he could hear were Mrs Baxter's footsteps fading as she walked away. Angrily, the kitten swiped the side of the box. Was that it? Why had she brought them here if she wasn't going to let them out?

'I'm hungry. When's Mum coming?' asked his black-and-white sister.

'I'm hungry too,' his other sisters echoed.

Mum wouldn't come. How could she? She wouldn't know where to find them. The kitten decided it was up to him to look after everyone. It was an exciting thought, but a scary one too. He stood tall, holding his tail up straight behind him.

'I'm in charge now. Let's get out of here! Then we'll look for something to eat.'

Reaching up, he tried to bat the lid open. He wasn't tall enough. He tried again, stretching right up, leaning his front paws against the side of the box and lifting his head to push it off. Still he couldn't quite reach. Full of frustration, he bunched his tiny body and jumped at the lid. His head batted it with a soft *thunk*. The kitten leaped again and again until suddenly the lid lifted, letting in a breath of fresh air and a rich woody smell. That was so good! Feeling encouraged, he sprang at the lid like a tiny tiger, bracing his body for the bump.

The lid of the box opened suddenly. Light and air flooded in as the kitten hurtled out. There was a surprised yelp, then two soft hands caught him round his middle, sweeping him

upwards until he was face to face
with a young girl. She had friendly
green eyes and long blond hair which
swept down her shoulders.

'Look!' she exclaimed, her mouth
widening into a smile. 'A kitten!'

2

Pixie

After changing out of her school uniform, Princess Katie went riding on Misty. Sitting back in the saddle she squeezed the reins, asking Misty to walk. Her eyes shone with happiness as she patted the pony's

dapple-grey neck. 'That was brilliant
fun. Can we do it again?'

Miss Blaze, the royal riding
instructor, laughed. 'Misty needs a
rest after all that galloping. We'll ride
this way tomorrow
if you like.'

'Yes, please,' said Katie eagerly. 'Tomorrow's Saturday, so we can stay out for longer.'

'What about your extra dance lesson?' asked Miss Blaze.

Katie scowled, then, remembering that wasn't very princess-like, quickly turned it into a smile. 'I'd forgotten about that. I'm learning a new dance to perform at Mum's birthday ball. Maybe if I do well today, Madame Quickstep will let me off her lesson tomorrow.'

Katie fell silent as she ran through the dance moves in her head. There was one really tricky bit, but she was good at dancing, so it shouldn't take long to get the hang of it. Deep in thought, Katie almost didn't notice the large cardboard box in the middle of the path.

'What's that?' she exclaimed, reining Misty in.

From inside the box came a funny squeaking noise and lots of scrabbling. Slipping her feet out of her stirrups, Katie jumped off Misty and handed her reins to Miss Blaze.

'Please look after us,' she said, reading the words written across the side of the box.

'Princess, wait! Let me open it,'
said Miss Blaze, hurriedly sliding off
her horse.

Katie was already lifting the lid.
She squealed in surprise as a bundle of
fur leaped into her hands.

'Look!' she exclaimed. 'A kitten!'

Holding the kitten up to her
face, Katie examined him. He was
a pretty silver-grey tabby with black
stripes, green eyes and pointed ears
that were a little too large for his
tiny body.

'Your ears make you look like a
pixie,' she giggled.

The kitten stared at her solemnly. The squeaking in the box was getting louder and he tried to wriggle free.

'What's that?' Tucking the kitten under one arm, Katie looked inside the box. 'More kittens! Oh, you poor things! Doesn't your owner want you any more? I'll have you! I'll have to ask my mum and dad first, but I bet they'll say yes, especially when they see how cute you are.'

Bending down, Princess Katie put the tabby back in the box so that she could stroke all of the kittens. They had silky-soft fur and long whiskers that tickled her hand, making her giggle. They were all eager for her attention, but the tabby was the boldest, mewing loudly and butting her with his head when she stopped stroking him.

'Princess Katie.' Katie looked up in surprise. Miss Blaze sounded worried. 'We have to go home.'

'Good,' said Katie. 'I think the kittens are hungry. How are we going to get them back? If I lead the horses, could you carry the box?'

Miss Blaze shook her head. 'The box is too big to carry that far. Besides, we'll be late if we walk.

Leave the kittens here and I'll come back for them in my car.'

Katie's stomach tightened in panic. 'We can't! They might escape. And what if someone else comes along? I've always wanted my own special cat. I'd really love to keep them!'

'It won't be for long,' said Miss Blaze gently. 'We'll put the lid back on the box so the kittens can't escape, and hide it safely in the bushes.'

'I'll wait here, then,' said Katie, scared that something bad might happen if they left the kittens on their own. 'Could you take Misty home for me?'

Miss Blaze shook her head. 'You know I can't do that. I'd be in very big trouble if I left you here alone.'

'But . . .' said Katie. She swallowed hard to stop the tears brimming in her eyes.

'It won't be for long. The kittens will be fine,' said Miss Blaze firmly.

Reluctantly, Katie patted each cat goodbye, leaving the little tabby until last.

'Be good, Pixie,' she whispered. 'I'll be back for you soon, I promise.' Wishing she didn't have to shut the kittens up again, Katie replaced the lid of the box. 'Where shall we hide them?'

'Over here,' said Miss Blaze, pointing to a large bush with huge red flowers.

Katie went over and, sinking to her knees, pushed aside the branches so that Miss Blaze could slide the box underneath the bush. She rearranged the leaves so that any passers-by wouldn't notice it hidden there.

Twigs snagged on her pink-and-lilac riding hat and her white jodhpurs got covered in dirt. Katie brushed as much of it off as she could before mounting Misty.

'Let's go,' she said, squeezing the pony into a fast trot.

The ride home seemed to take forever. Miss Blaze wouldn't let Katie canter because the ponies had worked hard and needed to cool down. Katie's heart leaped for joy when she glimpsed the huge silver turrets of Starlight Palace rising above the trees. She had lived in the palace all her life and always loved coming home, but she was especially pleased to see it right now.

She rode out of the woods, skirting the wide green lawns of the formal garden and taking the path that led to the stables. One of the peacocks was showing off, strutting along with his jewel-blue feathers outstretched. He looked amazing, but Katie was too worried about the kittens to pay him much attention. The moment she reached the stable yard, she jumped off Misty, ran her stirrups up their leathers and unbuckled the saddle.

'Hi, Katie. What's the hurry?'

Katie looked up and saw her best friend, Becky.

Katie and Becky were both nine years old and had known each other since they were babies. They saw each other almost every day. Becky's mum, Mrs Philips, was the palace housekeeper and her family lived in their own special rooms in the west tower.

'Hi, Becky. Guess what? I found a box of kittens abandoned in the woods! Miss Blaze is driving me back to get them. Do you want to come with us?'

'Kittens!' exclaimed Becky, pushing her curly brown hair out of her eyes. 'Really! What are they like?'

'They're so sweet. The box was too heavy to carry home, so we've hidden it. I just hope the kittens don't escape before we get back.' Katie's voice shook with worry and Becky squeezed her arm.

'Better hurry, then. You put Misty's tack away while I brush her down. I'll go and get her head collar and a dandy brush.'

'Thanks, Becky,' said Katie gratefully as her friend dashed away.

The girls made Misty comfortable then turned her out in the paddock.

Katie checked her watch. 'My dancing lesson is in forty minutes. That gives us plenty of time. We'd better go up to the palace and tell our mums where we're going.'

They ran through the gardens, ignoring the parakeets, who squawked angrily as they hared past, and scattering the red squirrels perched on the entrance to the maze. At the lake, they paused for a moment to catch their breath before crossing the rose garden and running

up the three flights of stone steps
next to the tiered lawns at the back
of the palace.

Suddenly, the patio door to the
family lounge swung open and the
queen stepped into the garden.

When Katie was in earshot, she
called out, 'Hello, darling, you're
back at last! The dressmaker's here.
She needs you to try your dress on
again. She's waiting for you in the
sewing room.'

Katie's face fell. 'I can't,' she
panted. 'I'm going back to the woods
with Becky and Miss Blaze to rescue
some stray kittens we found.'

'Stray kittens!' exclaimed the queen, her face wrinkling with surprise. 'But you've already got a cat.'

'Crystal's not mine, she's the royal cat,' said Katie. 'Please, Mum! I have to rescue these kittens. They're too little to be left alone.'

'I'm sorry, Katie, but my birthday ball is in two weeks. You have to go for a fitting or your dress won't be ready in time. Run along now, sweetie, and we'll talk about the kittens later.'

'But I've got my dancing lesson later,' said Katie, clenching her hands together.

'Come and see me after dancing then,' said the queen, going back inside and closing the door.

Katie's stomach tightened with fear. She couldn't disobey her mum but she had to save the kittens. Turning to Becky, she wailed, 'What am I going to do now?'

3

Missing

The little tabby kitten had loved
the girl with the soft hands.
He thought her name was Princess
Katie and she had called him
'Pixie'. She had been very good at
stroking. She hadn't pressed too

hard and she'd brushed his fur in
the right direction so that it lay flat.
She'd known exactly where to rub
him when he'd butted her hand
for more.

Pixie had sensed that Princess Katie
liked animals. She'd had two with
her, huge creatures with long legs and
a warm, sweet smell. The animals
had seemed to trust Princess Katie,
and Pixie had trusted her too. When
she placed him back in the box and
shut the lid, Pixie had thought she
was taking him home.

'What's happening?' his tortoiseshell
sister had squeaked in alarm.

'Shhh,' Pixie had mewed confidently. 'We're safe now.'

But Princess Katie hadn't taken the kittens home. Instead, she'd left the box in a dark place.

Pixie pressed his face against the side and peered through an air hole but not even a glimmer of light shone through it. Pixie could hardly believe it. What was going on? Why had Princess Katie left them? Anxiously, he paced round the box until his sisters complained that he was treading on them.

Pixie's stomach growled hungrily. If Princess Katie wasn't going to take the kittens home, then he'd better find food for everyone. Pleased to have something to do, he stood up.

'I'm going to get us something to eat,' he said.

Pixie jumped at the lid of the box, but, no matter how hard he batted it, he couldn't get it to stay open. Something seemed to be forcing it back. But he didn't give up. He kept going until, finally, after lots of jumping, the lid stayed open a little. Now Pixie could see that a branch was stopping it from opening properly. Crouching on the floor, Pixie sized up the gap. If he made himself very small, he might be able to squeeze through it. Using his black-and-white sister as a stepping stone, he reached up and hooked his claws over the side of the box. He hung on tightly and pulled himself up.

Pixie's bottom and tail swung wildly and his hind paws scrabbled against the box's side. He forced his head through the gap, panting, and he stayed there for a moment, catching his breath. Then, as he pulled up his back paws, he overbalanced and toppled forward. He reached out to save himself but he couldn't get a grip. Branches snagged at his fur, slowing him down until he landed in a pile of leaves with a soft *thud*.

Pixie's bones ached but, remembering what his mother had taught him, he sprang up and stared around, checking for danger. To his relief, there was none. Cautiously, Pixie forced his way through the bush until he broke out into the open. Ears pricked and whiskers twitching, he stood on the forest path and sniffed the air. There were so many new and wonderful smells. Pixie felt much braver now. Paws tingling with excitement, he set out to explore.

'Princess Katie, if you stopped
watching the clock and watched
where you were going, you might
learn this dance more quickly!'
said Madame Quickstep, the royal
dance teacher.

Princess Katie blushed. 'Sorry, Madame.'

'Let's start from the beginning. Go back to the middle of the room.' Pushing her glasses back on her nose, Madame Quickstep signalled for the pianist to start playing. Katie stood very still, listening to the opening bars of the music on the piano and counting herself in.

One, two, three and start. Gracefully, she stepped forward, lifting her arms out to the side and swinging her hips. *Step, two, three, turn, jump, jump, point. Shimmy across the room and jump again.* A picture of a tiny kitten with

pointed ears floated into her mind.
Unwillingly, Katie pushed it away.
She mustn't think about Pixie. If she
didn't get this dance right, Madame
Quickstep would never let her out of
the lesson.

Katie concentrated on her moves,
her gold dance shoes tapping out
a beat in time with the music.
She'd almost finished. Now for the
tricky bit: *run, leap and fly*. Landing
gracefully, Katie did a perfect
pirouette and came to a stop with
her hands high in the air.

'Bravo!' said Madame Quickstep,
clapping loudly. 'I knew you could

do it! We'll finish there and I'll see you tomorrow.'

'Thank you.' Katie curtsied to Madame Quickstep and the pianist, then hurried out of the room.

She ran down the corridor to the spiral staircase at the end. Katie's room was on the top floor of the south tower. There was a lift, but Katie preferred to use the stairs, especially when she was in a hurry. Kicking off her dance shoes, she raced up to the top floor and burst into her bedroom.

Katie had a round room with two huge windows that overlooked the lake. The walls were lilac and the ceiling was midnight-blue, dotted with tiny stars that sparkled in the dark. She had an enormous four-poster bed, hung with lilac and silver drapes, and a matching duvet and curtains.

Running into the large dressing room, Katie threw her shoes on the floor, unzipped her dress and removed her tiara. Katie loved dressing up, but today she wished that Madame Quickstep had let her dance in her jodhpurs. It would have been so much quicker. There was no time to put anything away, so Katie left her clothes in a heap and hoped Mum

wouldn't suddenly decide to inspect
her room. Princesses were supposed to
be tidy!

Katie's heart was pounding as
she ran back downstairs. Would
Becky and Miss Blaze be back yet?
Did they have the kittens with them?
What would they feed them? Not
the same cat food that Crystal ate,
that would be too rich for the kittens.
By the time she reached the stables,
Katie was gasping for breath. There
was no one about, but Miss Blaze's
green car was in the parking area.

'Becky,' called Katie, 'where are
you?'

'Here!' Becky poked her head out of the hay barn and waved Katie over. 'We've got them! Miss Blaze is just checking them over.'

Katie darted into the barn.

Miss Blaze was sitting by a cardboard box with the white kitten in her hand.

'Another girl,' she said, checking under her tail. 'She's a bit thin, but her eyes are bright, her nose is clean and she hasn't got any fleas.'

She held the kitten out to Katie. 'There you go. Four healthy kittens, all girls. '

'Four?' Katie took the kitten with both hands, supporting it carefully as she leaned over the box. Her heart sank like a stone. 'There's one missing!'

'I don't think so,' said Miss Blaze. 'There were only four kittens in the box when we collected it.'

An icy feeling swept over Katie. There had definitely been five kittens when she first found them. The white one she was holding, the little tortoiseshell, the cute grey-and-white one, the black one with the white tummy and paws – and Pixie, the silver-grey kitten with the black tiger stripes.

So where was Pixie now?

Katie began to tremble. 'We've got to go back to the woods,' she said. 'Pixie's missing!'

4

Mouse Hunt!

The great outdoors was even more exciting than Pixie had imagined. There were so many different sounds and smells! Pixie's ears and whiskers twitched non-stop as he took them all in.

A small creature fluttered past.
It flew a loop, then landed on a
clump of flowers. Pixie quivered with
excitement. What was that? On silent
paws, he crept closer. The thing had
pretty blue wings that kept opening
and shutting. It wouldn't make much
of a snack, but it looked fun to play
with. When the creature suddenly
took off, Pixie went after it. He
scampered along, leaping in the air as
it spiralled out of reach.

'Whiskers!' he squeaked, when
finally it disappeared.

Pixie wandered on, enjoying his
new freedom. The smells were so

much nicer than anything he'd ever
experienced before. As a particularly
delicious smell wafted towards him,
Pixie stopped, thrust his nose under
the bush it was coming from and
took a deep breath.

'Mmmmm!'

His mouth watered. Crawling
under the bush, he followed the
scent right to
the middle
and there
he found a
tiny animal
perched on
a branch.

Its beady eyes were bright with fear, its long whiskers trembling.

'Mouse!'

Mum used to bring mice home for the kittens sometimes. Unsheathing his claws, Pixie wriggled his bottom and sprang. There was a frightened squeak and a rush of air. The mouse vanished into the undergrowth, and Pixie crashed into the branch it had been sitting on and dropped to the floor. Leaping up, he gave chase until finally the mouse scurried up a tree. Experimentally, Pixie tapped the tree's trunk with a paw. Should he go after the mouse? It was a long way up. What if he got stuck or fell and hurt himself? Who would look after his sisters then? Reluctantly, Pixie let the mouse go.

The chase had made him very hungry. Knowing there were mice in the woods made Pixie determined to catch one for tea. He walked until his legs ached and his paw pads were sore. Plonking himself down on his bottom, Pixie gave himself a quick wash. That felt better. But if only he wasn't so ravenously hungry!

Looking around the unfamiliar space, Pixie realised the light was fading. It was time to go back.

If he was lucky, he'd catch a mouse on his way. Pixie stood up and stretched his legs. But which way *was* back? In the failing light, the forest looked the same in every direction. Pixie hesitated, unsure which way to go.

Princess Katie gently lowered the white kitten into the box.

'Please, Miss Blaze! We can't leave Pixie alone in the woods. He's too little.'

Miss Blaze ran a hand through her hair. 'Now you mention it, I do remember the tabby. He was the one that jumped out of the box when you first opened it.'

'Yes! That's the one,' cried Katie, excitedly.

'He must have somehow climbed out.' Miss Blaze sounded concerned. 'We'd better go and look for him. You two, go and wait in my car while I lock up the barn. We don't want the other kittens wandering off while we're gone.'

Katie threw herself at Miss Blaze and hugged her tightly. Then, remembering her manners, she quickly added, 'Thank you, Miss Blaze.'

Katie and Becky raced to the
car and, by the time the riding
instructor got into the driving seat,
they were sitting impatiently in
the back.

It didn't take long to drive to the
woods. Katie and Becky jumped
out of the car and ran on ahead.
They had no trouble recognising
the bush where the kittens had
been left. The ground
was covered with
footprints and
hoof marks.

Sinking to her knees, Princess Katie pushed back the branches.

'Pixie!' she called loudly. 'Pixie, here, kitty! We've come to take you home.'

Katie waited, her head tilted, as she listened for an answering cry or the patter of tiny paws. The silence stretched out around her. 'Pixie!' she called again.

'Did you find him?' Miss Blaze arrived as Katie and Becky were wriggling backwards out of the bush.

Katie's heart was hammering and her voice trembled as she answered. 'He's not here.'

'He can't have gone far,' said Miss Blaze briskly. 'Becky, you search over here, Princess Katie you search there and I'll take that bit.'

Everyone spread out. When they didn't find Pixie, Miss Blaze widened the search again. Katie's eyes were everywhere, from the dusty ground to the top of the trees. What if Pixie had climbed a tree and got stuck? If he had, Katie knew she would have to go after him, no matter how un-princess-like climbing trees was!

Scratchy branches snagged at her clothes and hair, but Katie hardly noticed. All that mattered was finding Pixie.

'Princess,' Miss Blaze came up behind Katie making her jump. 'It's time to go now.'

'But we haven't found Pixie,' said Katie with a worried frown.

'I don't think he's here,' replied Miss Blaze. 'He wouldn't have gone far. He's too little. Someone else must have found him and taken him home.'

'But what if they didn't? Pixie might be lost.' Katie swallowed as she struggled not to cry. 'Please, Miss Blaze, can we stay a bit longer?'

Miss Blaze shook her head. 'It's nearly teatime. You know we'll both be in trouble if you're not back in time. And what about the other kittens? They need to be fed. Pixie's an adventurous cat. I'm sure he'll be fine.'

Katie felt torn. Of course she had to get back and look after the other kittens – but what about Pixie? She couldn't bear to think of him alone in the woods at night.

'It's Saturday tomorrow, so no school,' said Becky suddenly. 'We could come back early. Before

breakfast, if you can make it? I bet
Dad would bring us if I ask him.'

'Would he?' Hope sparkled in
Katie's eyes. 'Yes, please, let's do that.'

Katie took one last look around,
then, linking arms with Becky, she
walked back to the car.

5

A New Home

'**W**e need to get some kitten food,' said Katie to Miss Blaze as they drove back to the palace.

'I've already sorted that out,' Miss Blaze replied. 'There were a few tins left over from when Crystal was a kitten and I've ordered in more for tomorrow.'

'What about dishes for the food and water?'

'You can use saucers for now. I expect Becky's mum has a stack of old ones somewhere.'

Becky nodded vigorously. 'She has. She hates throwing things away.'

Katie gazed out of the window and let out a big sigh. Where was Pixie now? She hoped that someone had found him and taken him home, but at the same time she felt terribly sad to think she might never see him again.

Arriving back at Starlight Palace, Becky ran off to ask her Mum for old saucers while Katie went to the kitchens to get the kitten food.

As she reached the barn, she met Becky, teetering under a stack of saucers. Miss Blaze opened the food and Katie and Becky spooned out small portions into four saucers, then poured the kittens some water.

The kittens mewed excitedly. Jumping out of their box, they rubbed their little bodies against Katie's and Becky's legs, making the girls giggle.

'They were starving!' Becky exclaimed as the black-and-white kitten pushed her empty saucer across the floor. 'Shall we give them some more?'

'That's enough for now,' said Miss Blaze. 'If you give them too much to eat in one go, they might get a tummy ache.'

We'll have to get a comb to groom them,' said Katie as they watched the kittens lick themselves clean.

Miss Blaze helped Katie and Becky carry the saucers to the stables and wash them up in the tack room. Katie rinsed out the sink then checked her watch.

'There's just enough time to move the kittens up to the palace,' she said.

'Where are you going to keep them?' asked Becky.

'In my bedroom.'

Katie was so excited about having her own kittens that she couldn't bear to be parted with them.

'You can come and see them whenever you like,' she added, knowing that Becky couldn't have a cat because they made her dad sneeze.

Miss Blaze offered to help the girls carry the box up to the palace.

'We'll use the lift to go upstairs,' puffed Katie as they entered the south tower.

But as they waited for the lift to arrive, the king appeared.

Miss Blaze and Becky curtsied. 'Hello, your majesty.'

'Hello, ladies. What's in the box – or is it a surprise?' asked the king.

'Kittens!' said Katie, proudly. She explained how they'd rescued them from the woods and how Pixie was still lost. Then she remembered that she hadn't been given permission to keep the kittens yet, and quickly added, 'I can have them, can't I, Dad?'

Thoughtfully, the king rubbed his chin. 'Kittens grow up. And we've already got a cat.'

'Crystal's the royal cat, not mine!' said Katie quickly. 'She's not very cuddly or friendly. Please, Dad, I promise I'll look after them and they'll be no trouble.'

The king laughed. 'I very much doubt that! Kittens are always trouble. They'll be into everything and they'll probably scratch the furniture. Remember what Crystal did to my throne when she was little? It was lucky the furniture maker was able to repair the damage.'

'I'll make sure my kittens behave and I'll get them a scratching post. Please, Dad, please let me keep them,' Katie wheedled.

The king pretended to sigh, then he ruffled his daughter's hair and said, 'All right, then. But they're not allowed in the palace. You can keep them in one of the barns.'

'But they're much too little to stay in the barns,' said Katie. 'And I'll hardly get to see them. If they share my room, I can make sure they're behaving.'

'You can't keep four kittens in your bedroom,' said the king firmly. 'How about you put them in the boot room? It won't matter so much if they make a mess in there.'

Katie really wanted to have the kittens in her room, but at least she was allowed to keep them. Shaking away her disappointment, she smiled and said, 'Thanks, Dad.'

Miss Blaze helped the girls carry the kittens to the boot room and then it was time for her to go. The kittens seemed very happy with their new home. The moment their box touched the ground, they jumped out to explore. The little tortoiseshell climbed inside one of the king's hiking boots and the white kitten squeezed in beside her. The grey-and-white kitten pounced on a trainer and tugged its laces. The black-and-white kitten attacked the hedgehog-shaped boot cleaner, batting it with tiny paws and squeaking in surprise when the hedgehog toppled over.

'That's so cute,' giggled Becky.

Katie's eyes shone. 'It's going to be such fun. We'll have to think up names for them too.'

'Bella for the black-and-white one,' said Becky. 'I don't know why, but it suits her.'

'It's perfect!' Katie agreed. 'Bella it is, then.'

Katie had a hard time dragging herself away from the kittens, but she couldn't be late for tea. Before she left, she made a note and stuck it on the door, warning everyone to keep it closed, to stop the kittens from wandering off.

'Bye, you beautiful kittens,' Katie said, giving each of them a kiss on the top of their head. 'I'll come and see you again later.'

Luckily for Katie, there were no visitors that evening, so tea was a relaxed meal with only two courses, eaten in the family's private dining room. Katie's little brother Alfie was very excited to learn about the kittens and wanted to see them. Katie and Alfie ate as fast as was polite and hardly tasted the delicious food – chicken, chips and sweetcorn followed by an enormous ice-cream sundae topped with strawberries and raspberries.

When the serving staff brought in the king and queen's coffee, Princess Katie asked if she and Alfie could be excused.

The king rolled his eyes. 'So a box
of kittens is more important than
spending time with your parents?'

Katie grinned. She knew he was
only joking.

It was fun showing the kittens to Alfie. Even though her six-year-old brother was often a noisy nuisance, Katie got on well with him most of the time. Alfie loved animals and was excellent with the kittens. He held them carefully, without squeezing them, and was very gentle when he stroked them.

'I like Bella, the black-and-white one, best,' said Alfie. 'Which one's your favourite, Katie?'

Katie looked at the kittens. Somehow it didn't seem right to have a favourite, but, if she was honest, she did have an extra soft spot for Pixie.

She wondered where he was now. What if he was still in the woods? Katie's heartbeat quickened and she swiftly pushed the thought away. But, no matter how hard she tried to ignore it, a picture of Pixie alone in the woods haunted her all evening.

Even when she was soaking in her huge round bath, full to the brim with strawberry-scented bubbles, Katie couldn't stop worrying about Pixie.

'It's no good,' she said, sitting up and reaching for the soap. 'I've got to go back to the woods!'

Katie bathed extra speedily. Wrapping a towel round herself, she padded from her en-suite bathroom into her dressing room. She put her nightie on then, returning her towel to the bathroom, she went to find her parents.

The king and queen were downstairs watching television, drinking large mugs of hot chocolate. They were most surprised that Katie wasn't in bed and even more taken aback that she wanted to go out to the woods.

'The kitten might not even be there, sweetheart,' said the king.

'But what if he is?' said Katie, her green eyes bright with tears.

The queen held out her arms to give Katie a hug. 'Mr Parks, the groundskeeper patrols at night. How about we ask him to look for your kitten?' she asked.

'That's a brilliant idea,' said Katie, pulling away. 'Can I go with him? I'm too worried to sleep and I don't have school tomorrow.'

The king and queen both laughed.

'Princess Katie, you're impossible!' said the king. 'I tell you what, if you promise to work extra hard at your dance and perform brilliantly at your mum's birthday ball, then just this once I will ask Mr Parks if you can go with him.'

Katie threw herself at her dad. 'Thank you, Dad! Can Becky come too, because I know she won't be able to sleep either?'

'You're totally impossible!' said the king, chuckling.

6

Alone in the Woods

Pixie had been walking for ages. Darkness was falling and, even though he could still see quite well, he went full circle three times, ending up exactly where he'd started.

Refusing to give up, he plodded on until at last he stumbled on a familiar path. This was the track he'd been looking for, the one that led to his sisters. Pixie was weak with hunger and tiredness, but success made him walk faster. Soon he reached the bush and, purring with delight, he called, 'I'm back!'

But, when he wriggled under the bush, he found it empty. The box had gone! Shocked and dismayed, Pixie stared at the ground. He was definitely at the right place. The earth smelt faintly of kittens. So where was everyone? The evening

breeze ruffled his fur and he shivered.
He didn't want to stay here on his
own. He wanted to be snuggled up
with his family.

Trying not to
panic, Pixie
scrambled back
onto the path
where he
nosed around
for clues.
There were lots
of prints on the ground.
Curiously, he sniffed at them. The
almost-round ones smelt of animal
but the other prints smelt of people.

Pixie's nose twitched with excitement as he examined the smallest human prints. These smelt just like Princess Katie, but some of them were newer than the others. Suddenly, he had a wild thought. What if Princess Katie had come back for the kittens? That had to be it! She must have returned when he was looking for food.

Food, grumbled Pixie's stomach. He was hungrier than he'd ever been in his life. He had to find Princess Katie! At first, it was easy to follow her trail. Even when there weren't any footsteps, Pixie could still detect her flower-like scent on the forest path.

He trotted on until the path opened
out into a huge rectangular clearing.
Pixie hesitated. It was harder to pick
up Princess Katie's scent here. There
were too many other strange smells,
including one that made Pixie's paws
tremble – the smell of dog. Mum
had smelt like that when she'd been
chased once.

There were no dogs here now,
though, thank goodness. Nose to
the ground, Pixie concentrated on
Princess Katie's scent, following the
trail into the middle of the clearing.

Pixie pawed at the ground in
surprise. He walked in a circle. Then,

lifting his nose, he sniffed the air.
Mysteriously, Princess Katie's scent
had vanished. Pixie was confused.
How could that happen? Unless
someone had put her in a box and
carried her off!

A strange hooting noise made
Pixie's fur stand up. He didn't like
the sound of that! Nervously, he
stared at the trees. There was a
soft rustle, then a large bird glided
silently towards him.

With a squeak, Pixie bolted. He
could feel the bird gaining on him.
His paws skittered across the ground
as he raced back to the forest.

Keep running – don't stop!

The bird was directly above Pixie. In terror, the kitten threw himself into the bushy undergrowth.

He curled up small, his heart hammering against his tiny chest. It was a long time before he dared to look up. The bird had gone but it had been a close call! Maybe he should stop searching for Princess Katie and wait until morning, when there would be less danger from night hunters.

Pixie settled down, but he was cold and lonely. He missed the cosy feeling of cuddling up with his sisters. Sadly, he curled his tail round his

body, sinking his nose into the fur to keep himself warm.

It took ages for sleep to come. The forest was alive with squeaks and rustles, and each one set Pixie's ears and nose nervously twitching. His stomach kept rumbling too. Pixie licked the ground, but it didn't taste very nice. He sighed. It was going to be a long night.

Princess Katie loved the palace gardens by night. The paths were lit by old-fashioned street lamps, and coloured lights shone in many of the trees and bushes. It was magical. But tonight, she was too concerned about Pixie to enjoy it. Clutching a large torch, she hurried along with Becky, Mr Parks and Mr Parks's dog, a friendly black Labrador called Sam.

'If the kitten's out there, Sam will find him,' Mr Parks said, confidently.

Crossing her fingers, Princess Katie hoped that he was right. She hadn't realised just how cold it was tonight. Pulling her fleece tighter, she was glad the queen had made her wear it over her dress.

It was very quiet. The peacocks and parakeets were in their aviary,

safe from foxes, and Katie felt as if she
should walk on tiptoe. She kept pace
with Becky, their joint torch beams
lighting up the path like a floodlight.
Every now and again, both girls
swept their torches wide of the path,
practising for when they entered the
dark woods to search
for Pixie.

'Don't go too far ahead!' called Mr Parks when Katie and Becky broke into a jog to keep up with Sam.

Katie wished Mr Parks would hurry up, especially when they left the formal gardens with its pretty lights behind and entered the woods. She also hoped the battery in her torch wouldn't fail. Princess Katie wasn't usually scared of the dark, but the squeaks and rustles of unseen creatures were making her stomach fizz with nerves. Catching hold of Becky's hand, she gave it a squeeze. Becky squeezed back and at once Katie felt ten times braver. But what

about Pixie? How would he feel if he
was alone in the dark?

We're coming to find you, Katie
silently told him.

7

A Long Night

They'd been out for ages and there was no sign of Pixie anywhere. Now Mr Parks was saying that in five minutes' time they'd have to go home!

'I don't think your kitten is here,' he said. 'He's probably tucked up in someone's home, fast asleep after a big tea,' he added kindly.

But Katie had a niggling feeling that Pixie wasn't safe. She walked more slowly, shining her torch down in the bushes, then up into trees, calling, 'Pixie!'

There was no answering cry.

Too soon, Mr Parks checked the luminous dial on his watch. 'That's it. Sorry, girls, but it's time to go back.'

He turned round, but Sam ignored his master's call to heel.

Nose pressed to the ground, he followed a new scent.

Katie swung her torch wide. Through the trees, she could just make out the car park she'd been to earlier with Miss Blaze. There were lots of animals in the woods and Sam had spent a happy evening tracking them, but this scent seemed to excite him more than any of the others. Wagging his tail, Sam left the path to nose around in the undergrowth.

Katie held her breath. What had Sam found? When Sam gave a surprised *Wuff*, Katie dived after him. Reaching down, she scooped up a tiny bedraggled bundle and hugged it close to her chest.

'Pixie,' she whispered. 'Thank goodness we found you.'

Pixie pressed his tiny body close to Katie's. His silver-grey fur was freezing cold and he was trembling with fright.

Katie unzipped her fleece, popped the kitten inside, then carefully zipped it up to his chin. 'You found him!'

Becky craned forward and Katie shifted so her friend could stroke the top of Pixie's head. 'Poor little thing, he looks so cold!'

'He's shivering,' Katie whispered. 'I hope he's going to be all right.'

It was a slow walk back. Pixie was so still that Katie kept stopping to check he was breathing.

'We might have to call the vet,' she worried.

'A cuddle and a bite to eat will bring him round,' said Mr Parks.

'Can you walk a bit faster, Princess? We don't want your parents to send out another search party for you!'

A while later, they entered through the kitchens, where Katie's mum was waiting for them. Even though Katie was worried about Pixie, she caught Becky's eye and managed a smile as they watched the queen spoon kitten food into a saucer for Pixie. It was a rare thing to see the queen in the kitchen! Becky took off her coat, but Katie kept hers on, leaving Pixie tucked inside as she continued to warm him up.

'Here you are,' said the queen, putting the saucer on the floor. 'Sit down, darling,' she added, pulling out a chair from the huge kitchen table.

Katie sat on the floor next to Pixie. At first, the little kitten ignored the food. *Please let him be all right!* thought Katie, as she nudged it closer. Pixie was too weak to take it, so Katie went and got a teaspoon. Putting some food on the spoon she nudged it at Pixie's mouth.

The food fell on the floor.

'Here,' said Becky, handing Katie a piece of kitchen roll.

Katie wiped away the spilt food and tried again.

'Come on, little Pixie,' whispered Katie. 'Don't give up, please!'

'You can do it!' Becky added softly.

Weakly, Pixie stared back at the girls and closed his eyes.

Katie nearly cried with despair. 'Please wake up, Pixie!' she murmured.

Pixie blinked, then slowly he began to eat. He stopped after a few bites, but Katie was ecstatic.

'Well done, you clever little kitten!' she said.

'He's a fighter!' said Mr Parks. 'With a bit of care he'll pull through. If I were you, I'd feed him every two hours tonight. That'll get his strength up. I can take him home and do it, if it's too much for you?'

'No, thank you,' said Katie, quickly. 'I can do it, can't I, Mum? I don't have school tomorrow.'

The queen smiled. 'You won't sleep if I say no, so I suppose that's a yes.'

'Thanks, Mum.' Katie smiled back gratefully.

At first Katie couldn't bear to put Pixie down. She'd lost him once and she didn't intend to lose him a second time. She cradled him in her lap, willing him to get better. But as the kitten began to feel warmer, Katie was persuaded to leave him while she ran up to her room with Becky so that her friend could change into her nightie.

Mrs Phillips, Becky's mum, had agreed that Becky could sleep over with Katie. Mrs Philips and the queen made a camp for the girls in a room near the kitchen with beanbags and blankets. They made Pixie a bed of towels next to it. Katie set the alarm on her watch for midnight, the time of Pixie's next feed.

Before she and Becky settled down
to sleep, they nipped along the
passage to the boot room together.
Quietly pushing the door open, the
girls peered inside. The other four

kittens were crammed in their bed, fast asleep.

'They're so sweet,' said Katie softly.

'They'll have such a surprise tomorrow when they see Pixie,' Becky whispered back.

'Yes,' said Katie, crossing her fingers because Pixie was still very weak.

At first, Katie and Becky lay on their beanbags, talking quietly so they didn't disturb Pixie. Every now and then, Katie checked that the kitten was all right. His tiny body felt so fragile, his heart fluttering like bird's wings. Gradually, Katie's eyes grew too heavy to stay open. Nestling into her beanbag, she pulled the blankets up to her nose and finally fell asleep.

Katie could hardly believe it when the alarm on her watch buzzed. Surely she'd only just closed her eyes! Sleepily, she got up. Pixie was still asleep, but Becky had woken too. Stifling yawns, the girls crept along to the kitchen to fetch more cat food. Pixie was still sleeping when they got back, but, when Katie leaned over his bed, the kitten woke up.

Katie was about to lift him up when she noticed Becky watching her longingly. She hesitated, then bravely asked, 'Would you like to hold him?'

'Me!' Becky flushed with pleasure. 'But Pixie's your kitten . . .'

'I don't mind,' said Katie, even though she minded badly. 'You do this feed and I'll do the next one. Sit down and I'll hand him to you.'

Becky was very patient with Pixie, but he hardly ate any of the food.

'He's still so weak,' said Katie, her face creasing with worry.

'At least he's warm now,' answered Becky as she carefully settled the kitten back down in his bed of towels.

Katie didn't sleep a wink after that. Lightly, she rested her hand on Pixie's soft fur as she watched him sleep. Every now and then, the kitten's paws twitched as if he was having a bad dream. The minutes crept slowly by. Katie wished the time would hurry so that she could try feeding Pixie again. He had to get his strength back! At a quarter to two she switched off the alarm on her watch and got up. It was no good –

she couldn't wait any longer! She woke Becky and they tiptoed to the kitchen for food.

When Katie scooped Pixie out of his bed, he stared right at her. Smiling back at him, Katie stroked his face. The kitten watched her with solemn eyes. Then, suddenly, he licked her hand.

Katie's heart leaped. Pixie was on the mend! As if agreeing with her, Pixie quickly ate the food Katie prepared for him.

'Aww, that's so sweet!' sighed Becky.

The girls shared a smile.

When Pixie had finished eating, Princess Katie hugged him to her. 'Hello, Pixie,' she whispered. 'Welcome to Starlight Palace, your new home.'

After two more feeds Pixie was almost back to his normal, bold self.

'Let's take him to see his sisters,' said Katie, yawning sleepily. She lifted Pixie up and he snuggled into her lilac dressing gown.

Quietly, the girls walked to the boot room. Becky pushed the door open.

'They're still asleep,' she said.

Katie put Pixie down. At first, he was a bit wobbly, but, after a few seconds, he sniffed the basket full of kittens. He stepped forward silently and suddenly pounced, landing in the basket on top of everyone!

The kittens scrambled up, squeaking and meowing with surprise. Katie and Becky couldn't stop laughing.

'Look, they're play-fighting,' giggled Katie, as the ginger kitten tugged at Pixie's tail.

Becky sighed happily. 'Having kittens is going to be such fun!'

'It's going to be brilliant,' agreed Princess Katie, giving her friend a hug. 'I can't wait to see what they'll get up to next!'

KITTEN FACT FILE

NAME: Pixie

COLOUR: A silver tabby with black stripes

EYES: Green

FAVOURITE FOOD: Fresh chicken

FAVOURITE GAME: Play-fighting with his sisters.
Pixie is a leader. He is the oldest of the kittens
and likes to look after his family.

SECRET FACT: Pixie is scared of the castle peacocks
but he's too proud to admit it.

Princess Katie's Top Kitten Tips

1. Put your kitten's bed in a quiet, draft-free place.

2. Make sure your kitten always has fresh water available.

3. Play with your kitten to keep it entertained. If you are going out then leave your kitten some toys to play with.

4. Keep food dishes clean by washing daily.

5. If your kitten has a litter tray then remove any soiled litter as soon as possible.

6. Don't leave uneaten cat food out. It can attract flies and they could make your kitten ill.

7. Kittens love to scratch so buy or make your kitten a scratching post.

8. Get your kitten microchipped
   by a vet – or other person trained
   to microchip cats. A microchip
   is a tiny device injected under
   your cat's skin that can be used to
   identify your cat if she gets lost.

9. Regularly treat your kitten for
   fleas and worms.

And finally, Katie's most important
tip of all:

10. Have fun with your kitten!

Princess Katie's Cool Cat Joke

Question: What is Pixie's favourite breakfast?

Answer: Mice Krispies!

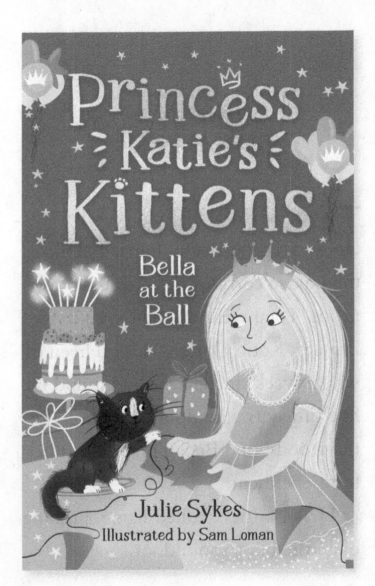

Princess Katie's Kittens

Bella at the Ball

Julie Sykes

Illustrated by Sam Loman

1

A Toy Mouse

Princess Katie of Tula and her best friend Becky hurried along the palace corridor towards the boot room. They were on their way to see Princess Katie's kittens. It had been a whole week since Katie had found the five tiny cats abandoned in a box in the woods, and Becky had helped her to rescue them.

'Hello, kitties!' called Katie, pushing open the boot-room door.

Immediately, Pixie, the silver-grey tabby, stopped attacking the laces of the king's walking boots and pranced over. He weaved round Katie's legs, rubbing his head against her.

Katie scratched him under the chin. Pixie purred ecstatically, then suddenly a black-and-white ball of fluff cannoned into him, knocking him over.

'Bella, you really are a cheeky thing!' Katie exclaimed.

Pixie sprang up and cuffed Bella with a paw. Bella batted him back and the two kittens rolled together on the floor.

'It's a good thing we don't play like that,' giggled Becky.

'Can you imagine what Dad would say?' Katie agreed. She made her voice go deep like the king's. 'Princesses never fight.'

Becky dug into her pocket and pulled out a felt mouse with a long string tail. The mouse jingled as Becky showed it to Katie. 'Look what Mum bought for the kittens. It's got a bell inside and it smells of catnip, which cats love.'

Becky put the mouse on the floor and pulled its long string. The mouse wiggled towards her. It looked so real that for a second Katie thought it had moved by itself. Immediately, Bella and Pixie stopped fighting and stared at the tinkling mouse. Then Bella pounced. But Becky was too quick, pulling the mouse just out of her reach.

'Look at her little face!' Katie couldn't stop laughing.

About the Author

As a child, Julie was always telling tales. Not the 'she ate all the cake, not me' kind but wildly exaggerated tales of everyday events. Julie still loves telling stories and is now the bestselling author of more than 100 books for children of all ages and is published around the world. She has recently moved to Cornwall with her family and a white wolf – cunningly disguised as a dog. When she's not writing she likes eating cake, reading and walking, often at the same time.

About the Illustrator

Sam Loman studied Illustration at the Academy of Arts in Rotterdam in the Netherlands (BDes) and Art, Design and Illustration at the University of Hertfordshire. She works full-time from her home as an illustrator/author for picture books and designs products like stationery, tableware, cards and more.

READ THEM ALL!